W9-BHL-139

Plumply, Dumply Pumpkin

Plumply, Dumply Pumpkin

written by Mary Serfozo

illustrated by Valeria Petrone

Aladdin Paperbacks

NEW YORK LONDON TORONTO SYDNEY

Also by Mary Serfozo

WHAT'S WHAT? A GUESSING GAME
illustrated by Keiko Narahashi

WHO SAID RED?
illustrated by Keiko Narahashi

First Aladdin Paperbacks edition September 2004

Text copyright © 2001 by Mary Serfozo
Illustrations copyright © 2001 by Valeria Petrone

ALADDIN PAPERBACKS
An imprint of Simon & Schuster
Children's Publishing Division
1230 Avenue of the Americas
New York, NY 10020

All rights reserved, including the right of
reproduction in whole or in part in any form.

Also available in Margaret K. McElderry Books,
Simon & Schuster Books for Young Readers hardcover edition.
Designed by Kristen Smith
The text of this book was set in Jam Loud.
The illustrations are digitally rendered.
Manufactured in China
6 8 10 9 7 5

The Library of Congress has cataloged the hardcover edition as follows:
Serfozo, Mary.
Plumply, dumply pumpkin / written by Mary Serfozo ; illustrated by Valeria Petrone—1st ed.
p. cm
Summary: Peter finds the perfect pumpkin so that he and his dad can make a jack-o-lantern.
ISBN 978-0-689-83834-7 (hc)
[1. Pumpkin—Fiction. 2. Jack-o-lanterns—Fiction. 3. Stories in rhyme.] I. Petrone, Valeria, ill. II. Title.
PZ8.3.S4688 Pl 2001
[E]—dc21
00-032421
ISBN 978-0-689-87135-1 (pbk)
0512 SCP

To Julie Dahlen,
a "real" librarian
—M. S.

Peter's looking for a pumpkin,
a perfect plumply, dumply pumpkin.

Not a lumpy, bumpy pumpkin.

Not a stumpy, grumpy pumpkin,
but a sunny, sumptuous pumpkin.

Finally on a twining vine
he spies a pumpkin fat and fine!

Not too fat, though, not at all.
Not too short and not too tall.

Not some squat, lopsided pumpkin,
but a glossy lot of pumpkin.

Why does Peter want a pumpkin?

Want a showy, glowy pumpkin?

Pumpkin pickles?
Pumpkin pie?

Pumpkin pudding?
Pumpkin fry?

Pumpkin salad?
Pumpkin stew?

What is Peter going to do?

With his pumpkin home at last,

Peter starts in working fast.

Draws some eyes and draws a chin,
then draws a plumply, dumply grin.

Helps his dad carve into place
a simply dimply, dumply face.

Lights a light behind the grin
to start it glowing from within.

Later wins the most
applause.
And really no surprise
because . . .

Perfect pumpkins really do make perfect jack-o-lanterns, too.